No Choice

Gloria Morgan

Published by

Dayglo Books Ltd, Nottingham, UK

www.dayglobooks.co.uk

0009-14-0713-03

Cover artwork & illustrations by
www.valentineart.co.uk

Typeset in Opendyslexic
by Abelardo Gonzales (2013)

Printed by IngramSpark

Distributed by Filament Publishing Ltd, Croydon

No Choice

CHAPTER 1

Craig kicked his school bag along in front of him all the way home. He held the bag up in front of him by the strap and gave it a jab with his toe every step he took.

Craig needed something to kick.

He was on his way home and that wasn't where he'd be going if he had any choice about it. Only he didn't.

School wasn't that great. He was in the rush with all the others to get out of the gates as fast as he could. But then the nearer he got to where he lived the slower he walked and the harder he kicked his bag.

Everything had gone wrong for him and his sister, Lisa, since people started dying.

He hated it when people died. It changed everything and there was nothing you could do about it. You could wish it was different but if someone died that was the end of it.

Arrangements got made, because they had to be, and you just had to get on with it. You had no choice.

He and Lisa had been brought up by their grandparents in a bungalow with a trim lawn and flower beds that were his Grandpa's pride and joy. When he wasn't mowing the lawn or weeding the borders, Grandpa would be pottering in his green-house, growing tomatoes.

Nanna cooked and washed and ironed and kept everything tidy and neat. She liked to be busy. Even when she was watching telly in the evening she would be knitting.

They lived with Nanna and Grandpa because their mum and dad had died in an accident when Craig and Lisa were very little, too young to remember anything about it.

It was never spoken of. If Craig or Lisa ever asked anything, Nanna would say never mind the past. Life was as it was today, and that was enough to be going on with.

Nanna and Grandpa were good to them and life had been all right in the bungalow until Grandpa got ill.

Nanna looked after him but he never got any better. Nanna said it was because he was old, and these things happened. They had to accept it and try to be good children.

That was the way Nanna talked. She told you

things without ever actually telling you any facts. Craig liked facts. You knew where you were with them.

You would have thought things couldn't have got worse for Nanna, with a sick husband and two grandchildren to bring up.

But things did. Grandpa got worse and then Nanna got cancer.

Just a few weeks after Craig and Lisa were told that, Grandpa was put in a home and they were standing side by side at Nanna's funeral, wondering what was going to happen to them next.

Their mum had been Nanna and Grandpa's only child.

They had just the one set of grandparents. They didn't know of any relatives on their dad's side.

It turned out, to their surprise, that their dad had had a cousin. He had been married but hadn't had any children and then he'd got divorced and no one knew where he was now.

But his ex, Auntie Joyce, offered Craig and Lisa a home with her.

Craig and Lisa weren't even sure exactly where she lived. Craig studied the road atlas, following the lines of the motorways. He looked at the names of towns. He'd never heard of any of them. It seemed like they were going to a foreign country.

Auntie Joyce lived on her own in this tiny one-bedroom flat. When they arrived that first weekend they bedded down in sleeping bags on the sitting room floor and stood up to eat their breakfast in her miniscule kitchen.

She was really nice and tried to make them feel welcome but it was obvious there simply wasn't room for them to live there with her.

Auntie Joyce's sister, Auntie Shirl, didn't have any children either but she had a husband.

Auntie Shirl and her husband lived in a big, shabby old house. There were a couple of spare rooms. Auntie Shirl said Craig and Lisa could stay there if they wanted.

What choice did they have?

CHAPTER 2

They had said yes to Auntie Shirl's offer and for the past two years they had been living with her and the man they called Uncle Pete.

And that was the trouble. Not the house. Not Auntie Shirl. It was Uncle Pete. And his cars.

The whole garden of the house was a graveyard of broken-down cars. Uncle Pete spent every waking minute tinkering with them, trying to repair them. They were his passion and his life.

Uncle Pete was not an easy-going man.

The only time he was happy was when he was messing about with his cars. For the rest of the time he was rude and grumpy and hardly ever smiled.

He preferred machines to people and the people he seemed to dislike most were his two lodgers.

Auntie Shirl was always all right with them but you'd have to admit she was no housekeeper. She didn't own a duster. Nanna would have been shocked at the dirty dishes piled in the kitchen sink and the state of the bathroom.

But the thing that upset Craig and Lisa was that Uncle Pete and Auntie Shirl argued all the time. The quarrels were getting worse and worse. They never stopped fighting. Everyone was feeling the strain of living under the same roof.

When Craig reached their house he stood hesitating at the gate.

He could see Uncle Pete, on his back, underneath a car he was fixing. He had spanners and other tools spread all round him. Uncle Pete, the car, and the patch of ground it was standing on, were all

coated with oil.

Craig watched Uncle Pete edge himself out

from under the car into the sunshine. He didn't notice

Craig at the gate.

It was a blustery day. Just at that moment

a sharp gust caught a load of dust and blew it square

in Uncle Pete's face.

Uncle Pete swore.

He sat on the ground rubbing his eyes,

grumbling. He didn't have a lot of hair, and what he

had was rumpled and dirty. He smoothed it down with

an oily hand, transferring more grit to the bald top of

his head.

Craig watched Uncle Pete stare round the

garden and wondered what he was looking for. He

soon found out. Uncle Pete got up and strode over to

the washing line.

Craig's duvet cover was hanging out to dry. Uncle Pete began pulling at it, not bothering to unpeg it.

Craig jerked into action. The gate slammed behind him as he dashed forward.

"Hey! What are you doing with that?"

"I need it to cover up me engine. Keep the dust out."

"Oh, no you don't!" Craig was furious. He grabbed hold of the corner, tugging with all his might. "You can't have that!"

"What!" Uncle Pete roared.

"It's mine. Let go!"

"Don't you talk to me like that!" Uncle Pete took a firm hold on the end, not loosening his grip.

"Auntie Shirl!" Craig was desperate. "Quick!"

Auntie Shirl stuck her head out of the kitchen door at the sound of Craig's voice.

"What's the matter?"

She came out into the yard and took in the situation. She caught hold of the corner nearest Craig's and began pulling with him.

"Tell him he can't have it, Auntie Shirl! He wants to put it over his car!"

"There's dust blowing everywhere and I've got to cover me engine!" Uncle Pete protested.

"Put it down! We got that for him for his birthday, special, remember! Put it down!"

Indeed, Auntie Shirl had gone to a lot of trouble to get the duvet cover for him. She'd had to send away for it.

It was all in shades of grey and brown. At first glance it seemed just a random pattern but when you looked closer you could see it was the heads of a dozen or more wolves. They were all different, with amazingly detailed, life-like faces, proud and fierce.

Craig was into wolves. Ever since that TV documentary. They were his thing. Craig loved his wolf duvet cover and would protect it with his life. Auntie Shirl remembered how much it had cost.

For a minute or two there was a three-way tug-of-war. Suddenly, Uncle Pete dropped the duvet cover with a curse, and it trailed in the dirt.

"That was clean and dry!" Auntie Shirl scolded, "Now it'll have to go back in the wash!"

Before she could lay her hand on it to return it to the laundry, Craig grabbed the cover, bundled it up in his arms, and ran off into the house with it.

CHAPTER 3

Craig opened his bedroom window and leaned out for some air. He didn't care about the dust blowing about.

He watched Lisa coming up the road on her way home from school.

As Lisa reached the back door, Uncle Pete followed her indoors with an arm full of car repair tools and oily rags. The back door banged shut behind them.

Craig turned from the window and threw himself down on his bed. He could feel the rage welling up inside him.

His wolf duvet cover had been a birthday

present. It meant a lot to him. And Uncle Pete was going to take it to put over his greasy old car engine. How dare he do that?

If Craig had got home five minutes later his duvet cover would have been gone for good. And if he'd complained, Uncle Pete would have told him not to be childish.

Him, childish! He was trying as hard as he could to act grown up. The one who was childish was the great, overgrown baby he had to live with, who didn't care about anyone else in the house.

Whenever he and Uncle Pete clashed, Craig always ended up wanting to punch something. He hated feeling like that and it made him so mad that Uncle Pete could do it to him, every time.

He reached for the remote and turned on his TV. Sitting in front of the TV in his room was the only place in the house where Craig could find peace. Nobody shouted back at you out of the TV screen. He could watch stuff that satisfied his curiosity, quiet and undisturbed.

For Craig, the Discovery channel was a life-line. He used to sit on the sofa and watch it with Grandpa. They had watched programmes about outer space and freak weather and poisonous snakes and old tombs that had never been opened in thousands of years.

Craig soaked up everything he watched and just wanted more. School was all right but they didn't tell you about all that amazing stuff.

For a bit, he channel hopped. Inside, he was still seething. He needed something to calm him down, something factual with lots of details that he could absorb himself in, to take his mind off Uncle Pete.

He was watching a programme about turtles

when Auntie Shirl called up the stairs:

"Come down, Craig. I want you."

He switched off the TV, heaved himself off the bed and left the sanctuary of his room.

"Uncle Pete wants fish 'n' chips for tea. Will you be a good boy and go and get them for us?"

"Oh, do I have to?" It was a horrible, cold, windy evening.

Auntie Shirl rummaged in her purse and handed him the money.

"Do I have to go, Auntie Shirl? If he wants fish, why can't he go?"

Uncle Pete appeared at that moment the back door, wiping greasy hands on his overalls.

"'Cos I've got more important things to do. I'm a motor mechanic, my lad, not a messenger boy."

Craig said nothing. He stuffed the money into his jacket pocket and set off.

There was a big queue when he got to the chip shop.

A man in striped chef's trousers and a white jacket came in from the back of the shop with a big metal bowl full of raw chips. He emptied them into the fryer and they sizzled in the boiling fat.

As the queue moved forward Craig shuffled to the counter and was served at last. The assistant scooped up four pieces of haddock and a pile of chips.

She wrapped each portion separately in a white paper package and enclosed the whole lot in the middle pages of last week's local free newspaper.

Craig set off home, cradling the warm, greasy parcel.

CHAPTER 4

Uncle Pete, Auntie Shirl and Lisa were watching TV when he got back. They each took a portion of fish and chips, helped themselves to salt and vinegar and ketchup and began eating with their fingers.

"Come on, Craig. Get yours."

Silence descended as they munched away.

Suddenly, without warning, the lights went out and the TV picture flickered and vanished. There was a chorus of angry protest from the family.

"Oi, we were watching that!"

Craig wouldn't have been surprised to see Uncle Pete kick the TV in temper.

Lisa jumped up and went to the light switch

and flicked it on and off, but nothing happened and they were left sitting in the dark.

Auntie Shirl went into the kitchen and tried switching things on. Nothing worked.

"All the power's off."

Uncle Pete swore.

"Oi, not in front of the kids!"

Uncle Pete kicked the table leg.

"Get on with your supper. Finish it before it gets cold," Auntie Shirl told the children.

"Auntie Shirl, can we light that candle we had at Christmas?" Lisa asked.

"What a good idea, darling."

The little wax Father Christmas was fetched to the table and given pride of place, where the flame cast its glow over a surprisingly wide area.

"This is fun." Lisa was enjoying the novelty of a candle-lit supper.

Uncle Pete grumbled into his battered haddock.

Craig, meanwhile, reached across and picked up a sheet of newspaper that had been wrapped round their supper. He held it close to the candlelight.

Auntie Shirl went out into the kitchen to boil a pan of water on the gas, to make a cup of tea.

A shriek went up in the sitting room as she was coming back with the first two mugs of tea.

One of the kids – according to Uncle Pete – had knocked the squeezy bottle of tomato ketchup off the table. He'd got up to find it and in the dark he'd stepped on it and squirted tomato ketchup all over the carpet.

Auntie Shirl back-tracked to get a cloth to mop up.

"You knocked that on the floor, Lisa! You want to be more careful!"

"I didn't, Uncle Pete!"

"Well then, it was you, Craig!"

"Wasn't me!"

"You're always on to those kids. Leave them alone for once, will you?" Auntie Shirl's patience was running out.

"They're useless, the pair of them!"

Craig winced. It was horrendous being cooped up with Uncle Pete like this. You could taste the tension in the room. Craig reached for the newspaper again and buried his head in it.

Uncle Pete screwed up the last of his chips in a twist of wrapping paper and lobbed it into the empty fireplace.

"What you do that for?" Auntie Shirl demanded. "We aren't going to light a fire in there for months."

"I'm going to light a fire tonight," Uncle Pete retorted. "Give me your paper, then," he instructed.

They each handed him their greasy wrappers. Uncle Pete squatted down and put them in the empty grate.

"Give me the candle."

Lisa passed it to him.

"Don't set fire to Father Christmas, will you."

Uncle Pete glared at her.

"You think I've never lit a fire before?"

"No, Uncle Pete."

"Shut up, then."

He held the candle to the nearest edge of paper and it caught in a moment.

Craig had put his page of newspaper down to have a drink of tea and before he could go back to it, Uncle Pete reached across and grabbed it and added it to the flames.

Craig was livid. This time Uncle Pete had gone too far.

"Hey! I was reading that!"

Craig felt a burning fury inflating like a balloon inside his chest until he thought it would burst right out of him. He had to do something or he would explode.

He stamped from the table and banged out into the kitchen. A moment later he was back, clutching a handful of Uncle Pete's oily rags behind his back.

He stormed to the fire place. Uncle Pete was still squatting down, watching the chip papers blaze. Craig tossed the rags into the fire.

Instantly, the flames doubled in volume and roared angrily up the chimney. At the same time they billowed out into the room.

Uncle Pete was knocked flat on his back, with a cry. He scrambled to his feet with difficulty. He clutched the furniture with one hand, and dabbed at his eyebrows with the other.

"You . . . you . . . you flamin' set light to me!" he roared.

As soon as he had lobbed his missile, Craig turned tail and raced up to his bedroom and barricaded himself in.

Without thinking, he touched the light switch but, of course, nothing happened. No power. So no TV to get lost in, until the turmoil was over.

He heard Uncle Pete chase him up the stairs.

"You come out of there! I'm going to tan the hide off you!"

Uncle Pete rattled the door knob till Craig thought he was going to pull it off.

Craig flung himself down on his bed in the darkness. He hugged his duvet cover to him and buried his face in his pillow.

Eventually, Uncle Pete retreated down the stairs, still uttering angry threats.

CHAPTER 5

Some time later Lisa tapped quietly at the bedroom door.

"Craig, it's me. Let me in. I'm on my own."

He moved the chair away from under the door knob and opened up for her and she quickly slipped inside. Craig put the chair back under the door handle.

"Are you all right?" Lisa had never seen her brother so incensed.

"Yes. I'm okay. You?"

"I suppose so. But I tell you this, Craig, I'm fed up to the back teeth with all this fighting."

"I know. It's horrible, isn't it."

"They're at it again now. I can't stand it. This is the last time I'm going to be piggy-in-the-middle while Auntie Shirl and Uncle Pete have a row. I've had enough. I'm out of here."

"What? You mean you're going to leave?"

"Yes."

"Where would you go?"

"To Auntie Joyce's. She'd have us."

There was a pause.

"You'd come with me, wouldn't you Craig? We can get out of my bedroom window. Then we can run to the bus stop. I've got money. Come on – shall we do it?"

She waited in the dark a long time for his voice:

"All right. Okay."

Craig followed Lisa into her room and they helped each other scramble out of the window on to the garage roof below. They crawled across it on hands and knees, getting very dirty in the process. It was quite a jump down to the ground but they did it.

Then they ran as fast as they could to the nearest bus stop. It was only a few minutes before a bus came along. They got on, and stayed on until the terminus.

"Do you know where we are, Lisa?"

"No, but it's a main road. We must be nearly at Auntie Joyce's."

The area seemed familiar but nothing stood out as a landmark Lisa could quite recognise. The shops were similar, but not exactly the same as those she knew near Auntie Joyce's house.

They made their way down the road, looking into shop windows, hoping to see a clue to tell them where they were. The post office, the dry cleaner, the card shop, none of them quite rang a bell.

The day was fading into evening. They wandered on past more shops, a pub, a row of terraced houses.

The only other building nearby was a big, old ruin of a house, surrounded by an overgrown lawn.

"I wonder who that place belongs to," Lisa said. The house looked deserted.

"Dunno," Craig shrugged.

I bet nobody lives there."

"It definitely isn't Auntie Joyce's."

Beyond the big house there was a small, wooden building, like a summer house.

"Let's go and have a look in there," Lisa suggested.

She walked across and peered in through the window. Craig peeped over her shoulder. Lisa tried the door. It wasn't locked.

To their surprise, it was dry and snug inside.

There were curtains at the window, two folding

garden chairs and a little table.

"Why don't we stay the night here?" Lisa

suggested. "Then we can ask directions to Auntie

Joyce's in the morning."

CHAPTER 6

"Might as well make ourselves comfortable." Craig unfolded the chairs and they sat down.

He noticed a fancy, metal holder with candles in, hanging down from the ceiling. He searched around and found some matches on the table and lit the candles.

"This is all right," Lisa declared, in the soft, yellow glow, "having a little house to ourselves."

They were quite unprepared for a knock on the door five minutes later.

"Who is within?" called a quavering voice.

Lisa's heart skipped a beat.

The door opened. On the threshold stood an

old man, tall and very wrinkled, wearing a faded brown velvet suit. He stood staring at them.

Lisa and Craig hastily got to their feet.

"Er . . . sorry . . . we thought it would be all right to sit down . . ."

"What do you want?" the man asked.

"We were trying to find our way to our Auntie Joyce's . . ."

"We didn't mean any harm . . ."

He nodded slowly.

"No. No. Of course you didn't." He seemed to be satisfied that they hadn't come intending to break into the house and rob him.

"Very few find a path to this door," he explained in a wheezy tone, "But you are welcome to come inside. Follow me."

The old man turned abruptly and started to walk across the lawn towards the house.

Lisa couldn't believe it.

"He surely doesn't live in there? It looks as if it's falling down."

"If he says we can go indoors, I suppose he must live there. Come on." Craig set off.

The old man led them round to the front of the house and in at the main entrance.

The place looked so off-putting from the outside, they could hardly believe the difference once they were through the door.

The hall floor was tiled in blue and green. Wide, carpeted stairs went up to the left. Ahead, the hall led off into darkness beyond the staircase. To the right, a door stood open.

"Come in."

The old man ushered them into the room and left them there, alone.

They stared round in disbelief. It was like the

lounge of an old-fashioned hotel. There was an open coal fire burning, with a table beside it, and two sofas with thick, squashy cushions.

At the windows, heavy curtains hung to the floor. There were pictures and mirrors in ornate frames on the walls.

A grandfather clock in the corner kept time with a deep, regular tick. The only other sound was the soft crackle of the fire.

The room was clean and tidy, as if guests were expected.

They weren't sure whether they should sit down so they stood waiting for the old man to come back.

"You may stay for the time being," he told them, in a croaky voice, when he came in again.

"Thank you." Lisa was glad not to be getting into trouble for going inside the summer house.

"Do you live here all by yourself?" Lisa asked the old man.

Craig nudged her: "Don't be so nosey."

"No. No. I am merely the butler. The house belongs to my mistress. I have served her for many years."

"Who is your mistress?"

"She is a lady of advanced years – as am I, indeed. She was formerly a ballet dancer."

"Really?"

"Oh, yes. My mistress was a legend – people came from far and wide to see her dance. Sadly, there came a day when my mistress could no longer dance. She became ill and could not go out. Now she spends her days confined to her room and I wait upon her as best I can."

Craig suddenly caught sight of himself in a mirror on the wall. He had dirty smudges all over his face and hands. He must have got those when they

crawled across the garage roof.

"Excuse me, but do you have somewhere

I could have a wash?"

"Certainly. Come with me."

CHAPTER 7

The old butler hobbled up the stairs, and led them to a large, tiled bathroom.

In the corner was a vast, marble bath tub with gold taps, an old-fashioned shower and a thick shower curtain. There were piles of white, fluffy towels.

"I'm going back downstairs" Lisa announced.

Craig had a good look at everything in the bathroom before he started to get undressed.

Like in the sitting room, everything was old, but cared for. There were countless bars of soap, tubs of cream, and bottles of shampoo.

Craig got into the big, oval bathtub, closed

the curtain and activated the shower. It was

a vigorous jet and the bathroom was soon thoroughly

steamed up.

Craig decided to try all the different soaps and

shampoos. The sudsy smell and the pounding of the

hot water on his skin were wonderfully relaxing. It

was just what he needed after the day he'd had.

Craig tipped his head back. He breathed in

deeply and let out all the air in a big sigh. It felt

good. He closed his eyes.

Suddenly, the water began to run cold. Craig

reached forward to adjust the control, but he lost his

footing and slipped and fell. He splashed about,

trying to stand up again, but he couldn't.

Something strange and scary was going on.

Craig was no longer enjoying a shower. He was out of

doors, in the pouring with rain, swimming for his life

in icy cold water.

He looked round frantically, trying to see where he was, but visibility was almost nil. He seemed to be in a wide river at the bottom of a deep canyon. He could feel himself being swept along on a terrifyingly strong current.

Not far ahead, he could hear the sound of rapids as water churned over the lip of a waterfall.

He caught sight of a length of rope in the water and reached out desperately to grab it. To his relief, he managed to reach it and hang on, and it halted his breakneck progress, at least temporarily.

"Wherever am I? What am I going to do? How am I going to get back to Lisa?"

Craig considered himself a fair swimmer, but that was in the local pool. He could barely keep afloat in these turbulent waters.

It was impossible to see more than a few feet in front of his face for the torrential rain.

He was very frightened. He clung on as long as he could, but gradually exhaustion set in. He felt the rope slipping but there was nothing he could do.

He was struggling to keep his head above the water. The undertow was so strong that however hard he kicked his legs he couldn't swim against it.

Gradually, inexorably, he was being dragged nearer and nearer the rim of the waterfall.

"Lisa, where are you?" was his last thought as the torrent overwhelmed him and he was swept over the edge, cart-wheeling down, tossed this way and that, in a blur of noise and speed.

The water was travelling so fast that it felt like a solid wall. Craig was bumped and bashed against it as he fell.

It was a wild, headlong, unstoppable descent – down, down, down what felt like the deepest waterfall in the world.

CHAPTER 8

Craig's descent came to a jarring halt. At the extreme far edge of the waterfall, near to dry land, a slender tongue of stone protruded from the cliff side, through the raging torrent. It sent jets of spray spurting up into the air. They cascaded back in liquid rainbows, as they rejoined the descending waters.

Craig's body hit this stone and was deflected to the side, out of the path of the main flow.

Bruised and winded, he lay for a long time where he fell, half submerged. He drifted in and out of consciousness.

In his occasional lucid moments, his head thrumming and every bone aching, he tried, without success, to remember what had happened to him, and guess where he might be.

The incessant, thundering noise of the water-fall forced itself into his awareness. He revived enough to raise his head and stare around him.

Looking up, the sight of the torrent bearing down on him and passing close enough to soak him, made him catch his breath. He pressed back hard against the stone beneath his shoulders.

When he turned his head and looked down, vertigo hit him in a sickening spasm.

He closed his eyes, convinced he was about to spin off the narrow ledge into the churning waters below.

He lay there shaking, his teeth chattering, paralysed with dread.

The roaring of the falls drowned out any other sound, any other thought.

Debris of all sorts came hurtling down. Half a tree, with leaves still clinging to the branches, came dangerously close to him. It threatened to dislodge him from his precarious perch.

The constant movement, the constant noise, and the swirling currents of air caused by the rush over the rim, were more than his senses could cope with. He was dizzy, fainting. He lay in a stupor.

Some sixth sense penetrated the barrier of his fear and nausea. As a little life gradually seeped back into his battered body, his brain began slowly to function again, and he realised, however dully, that he was no longer alone.

As impossible as it seemed, in the middle of that maelstrom, another living thing was nearby, next to him, close enough to touch him.

He had no idea who it could possibly be. All his instincts told him to try to get away.

Panic overtook him as he struggled in vain to move limbs that disobeyed him. He was powerless to stir, held down by the dead weight of his exhaustion and terror.

He could hear muffled noises in his ear, feel breath on his face. Then he felt the pressure of a muscular body leaning against his, pushing him back from his perilous position on the edge of the rocky spur.

Next, powerful jaws took hold of his shoulder and holding it firmly, but not too hard, tugged at it. With no strength to protest, he whimpered, and then he felt his leg taken hold of.

Little by little, he was pulled from where he had fallen and set down again a few yards away.

Desperate to know where he was, he summoned up the courage to peep.

He found he was now on a wider ledge of rock,

away to the side of the waterfall. The noise was still as bad, and he could see a solid sheet of water hurtling down, only a short distance away.

But here, he was out of immediate danger of being swept over the brink.

With relief, he quickly shut his eyes again. He had no idea who had rescued him, or why, but he knew they had braved great danger to reach him and drag him to safety.

He strained his ears to try to catch a clue as to who had come to his aid. He tried to move his head, but he could not. Finally, he opened his eyes.

CHAPTER 9

Craig was surrounded by wolves. Huge wolves. Wolves bigger than he had ever imagined.

All he could see from where he lay were their legs, thickly covered with coarse dark fur, and their enormous paws. There seemed to be about a dozen of them, ranged around him in a circle. In their grey faces burned wary yellow eyes.

In spite of himself, Craig let out a gasp.

"Ah – so you are awake," said the one whom Craig guessed must be the leader. The voice had a thick, unfamiliar accent but it didn't strike Craig as at all odd that he could understand him. In reply, he blinked, too weak to nod.

"Good. You were lucky to survive your fall."

Craig blinked again, heartily agreeing with him.

"I am Nurek. You are of our kind. We will take you with us."

What did that mean? What kind of what? Where were they going to take him?

Immediately, several of the wolves leaned down and nudged him on to what felt like a piece of sacking. Then two of them grabbed the front corners and began to drag it along. They were so much bigger than him that it was no problem for them to haul him behind them.

He was bumped and bounced about so much he was afraid he would slide off his mat, but they did not let him fall. From time to time, at a signal from Nurek, they would pause and change position, so that a fresh pair was towing Craig along.

Their journey took them from the edge of the

falls deep into a forest of tall trees. The light under

the branches was gloomy and pine-scented. There

were well-worn tracks winding between the tall

trunks and the pack ran faster here.

Craig couldn't tell how long they ran, but he

guessed they travelled a long distance. The woods

were quiet and the sound of the waterfall faded to

a distant murmur.

At last they slowed down and, on Nurek's

instructions, let go of their burden. Craig was grateful

that the jolting had stopped. He glanced around.

They were in a clearing and, to his surprise,

they were outside a rough wooden cabin.

It looked as if it has been made from the

trunks of tall thin trees, laid one on top of the other,

exactly as they had been felled, and lashed together

with lengths of stringy vegetation. There was a door,

held on with hinges plaited from the same material. Craig wondered who lived there.

"This is where we shelter our cubs and our old and sick," Nurek explained. "You shall have refuge here until you are strong."

Without waiting for any response from Craig, two of the dogs came forward and took up the corners of his mat again, while another opened the door.

Craig was drawn inside and deposited, with his bed, in the middle of the floor. Then the wolves went outside again and the door swung shut behind them. No sound penetrated the thick wooden walls.

Craig peered round to try to get his bearings. There was a small window high up in the wall, opposite the door.

As his eyes grew accustomed to the dim light he could pick out the shape of a wolf asleep on a pile of dry leaves in the corner. In the other corner lay

a female wolf with a litter of new-born pups. She was

awake and looked over with curiosity, but made no

sound.

Craig was glad the long, uncomfortable ride

was over. He was grateful to his rescuers but now

wanted only to be left alone.

The hut was warm and dry. There was no noise

apart from the steady breathing of the sleeper and

the snuffles of the pups.

Craig was tired out. Nothing further seemed to

be expected of him, so he made himself as

comfortable as he could and in two minutes was

sound asleep.

CHAPTER 10

When he woke it was dark. He wondered how long he had slept. Tentatively, he stretched out his legs and arms. He was surprised to find that, apparently, no bones were broken. But he was unbelievably stiff and his limbs felt as though they didn't belong to him.

He shifted his weight and tried to ease his aching back. To his surprise, a voice spoke out of the darkness.

"Hello." It was the female with the pups. She had the same heavy accent as Nurek.

"Hello. I'm sorry, did I wake you?"

"No. I was awake. How are you feeling?"

"Not too bad. I don't think I've broken anything but I've got plenty of bruises."

"I'm not surprised. Nurek told me you'd gone over the falls."

"That's right."

"You're lucky to be alive."

"Yes, I am. And lucky someone found me. When I opened my eyes and saw where I was, half way down the waterfall, I was too scared to move. But someone came and rescued me. They must be very brave."

"That was Nurek. He is our leader. He is also the father of my cubs. He is the bravest wolf in the wilds."

Craig knew a bit about wolves from the TV. He tried to remember programmes he had seen. They were mostly to do with wolves ripping and devouring and yowling and baying.

They were portrayed as aggressive brutes that would kill anything they saw and ask questions afterwards. And yet they had not hurt him.

Vulnerable and half-dead as he had been, Nurek had told the pack to bring him here, and sheltered him. It seemed these wolves were different.

He dropped to sleep again and when he woke it was morning. The mother of the cubs was busy feeding and washing them. They were plump and wriggly, always hungry, and they kept their mother busy.

She told Craig her name was Garell and that she had given birth to two males and a female.

They would stay in the cabin with her for ten days, until their eyes were open. After that, Garell would return to the pack and the cubs would learn to live out of doors.

Craig tried to get to his feet, couldn't, and
flopped down again. He felt really odd. His limbs felt
heavy and awkward, like they had in the night, only
worse. And itchy. Like nothing he could remember
feeling before.

In the dim daylight from the window he took
a closer look. Gingerly, he pushed his bedding aside
and stared down at his limbs.

All his body, his head, his arms and legs were
covered in thick, pale grey fur. Except his arms
weren't arms any more. They were legs.

Four legs and a fur-covered body. He was not
looking at a boy, but a small, pale grey wolf.

It was a beautiful moment. Suddenly Craig
knew he was where he was meant to be. The wolves
were his kind and he was theirs. One small member
of a great wolf family.

CHAPTER 11

At that moment Nurek came in, dragging a piece of raw meat for Garell. Another of the wolves followed with a smaller hunk and offered it to Craig.

Craig had never eaten raw meat before. He didn't know what to do. But he was hungry and the other wolves were watching him. Best not hesitate for too long or they might suspect something.

The first bite tasted so good he demolished his portion in very few mouthfuls.

He couldn't believe he had done that, when he stopped to think about it afterwards.

"Garell, where does the meat come from?" They were alone after the meal.

"We hunt and kill our meat ourselves. Sometimes we catch fish, too."

Craig sat and thought about hunting for food. He wouldn't know where to start. Auntie Shirl always put his meals on the table for him. It was usually pizza or fish from the chip shop. They did sometimes have meat, like at Christmas.

"Garell, what was the meat we've just eaten?"

"Deer. Did you like it?"

"Yes, it was good. Do you often have deer?"

"When we can get it."

"What do you eat when you can't get deer?"

"Rabbit, sometimes. But deer is better because there is only one meal on a rabbit but many can feed from a deer."

"Is it hard, catching a deer?"

"We use our intelligence and we work as a pack. Six wolves hunting together can bring down an animal much larger than themselves."

"Does anybody hunt wolves?"

"Only men."

"Men? Why?"

"Men hate wolves. They say that we kill their livestock. They even accuse us of stealing babies from their cradles. But this is a lie. Wolves leave men alone, keep to the forests, hunt only wild beasts. Wolves are proud and noble creatures. We avoid men whenever we can."

"Tell me about the pack."

"We belong to the pack for life. Our leader is the strongest, bravest and most quick-witted wolf. All the others swear loyalty to him, but they are themselves fearless and clever.

"We trust each other, hunt together many times, use the skill of each member of the pack. There is strength in numbers, but more strength in such intelligence and teamwork. This is how the pack survives and thrives."

"Doesn't anyone ever leave the pack?"

"When a leader is becoming old, one of the young males will challenge him. If he is mistaken, and the old leader is still strong and can beat him in single combat, then the young male will leave and go away into the wilderness and perhaps set up a new pack of his own elsewhere. But otherwise, no. We stay always together."

"And what happens if the young male wins the contest?"

"He takes over as leader of the pack."

"What about the old leader. Does the young leader kill him?"

"No, of course not!" Garell was shocked. "Wolves do not kill other wolves. An old leader will know when the time has come to step aside. He will not put up a great fight, but he must present some obstacle to the younger wolf, otherwise how can he prove to the pack that he is fit to rule them?"

"Does the old leader have to leave the pack?"

"No. He bows to the younger leader and takes his place lower down in the order, keeping the oath of loyalty to the pack that he swore in his own youth. He will run with us and hunt with us until his dying day."

Craig had a deal to think about as he curled up on his mat. Now he had become a wolf there was so much he needed to know. He was glad they brought him into the hut where he could ask Garell all his questions.

But what was his position in the eyes of the pack. Was he a guest or a prisoner?

CHAPTER 12

As the bruises faded, Craig began to experiment with his new body. He was amazed how easy it was to walk on four legs. To his own surprise, he adapted quickly to his new diet. But although he could eat like a wolf and move like a wolf, he still thought like a boy.

He explored every inch of the cabin. The only furniture was a low, three-legged stool made of rough timber, lashed together with twine.

The old wolf who occupied the corner did very little except sleep and occasionally eat a little. He was not talkative at all and it was Garell who told Craig his name was Lurrar.

He had once been leader of their pack,
a formidable champion in his day who was greatly
respected in his old age. Her cubs would be taught
what an honour it was to have been born and raised
in his presence.

"Garell, who built this cabin?"

"Men, many moons ago. Once they used to
come from the village to fell timber. They built this
place. But no one comes now. We saw it was
deserted, and one hard winter we began to use it to
shelter against the harshest weather. When men
realised that we had been in here, they never came
back."

Craig remembered what Garell had said about
irrational hatred and prejudice. Why would the men
not come back after the wolves had been in the hut?
What were they afraid of?

Next day the door opened and one of the

younger wolves came in but this time he was not bringing food, but a message for Craig that Nurek wished to see him.

Craig followed the messenger outside, glad to be going out into the fresh air at last but none too sure what Nurek wanted him for, and afraid that it would not be for anything good.

His guide brought him into Nurek's presence and left him, stepping back immediately into the shade of the trees.

Nurek sat alone in the middle of the clearing outside the cabin. Craig stood before him awkwardly, not knowing what to say. Nurek looked at him long and hard before he spoke:

"I do not know how you found your way here, but the choices for you, now that you are here, are few. None but wolves live in these forests and, as you know, we live in our own packs. One small stranger would find it hard to survive alone."

He paused. Craig held his breath.

"However," Nurek continued, "although you are not truly one of us, you are of our kind. Could you live with us?"

"I think so. I could try." That was as far as he dared commit himself. Whether he could succeed would depend on more than Nurek could imagine.

"And would you pledge your loyalty to me, as your leader?"

Craig remembered Garell's words. If Nurek did not have his oath, he had no future.

"I would."

"Would you trust me with your life?"

"Yes, I would." This was the wolf who had already saved him from otherwise certain death.

"And should I entrust my life to you?"

"Yes." He answered quickly, realising that hesitation would seem disrespectful, although he hoped with all his heart he would never have to accept such responsibility.

"If you pledge yourself to me, you must also prove yourself to our pack. Then we will accept you as one of our own."

Craig bent his head very low in a gesture of submission:

"That would be a great honour."

He sensed he had answered well and his response had pleased Nurek.

"In order to be admitted into the pack, you will have to undergo an initiation. Are you ready for that?"

"I am." Craig had no option but to agree, despite having no idea what he was agreeing to. He was sure he would find out soon enough.

"Good. Good," Nurek nodded. "You will need to prove yourself to us through your courage and endurance. Can you do this."

"Yes." What on earth would he have to do?

"Tonight, from the hour when the sun sets, until tomorrow, at the hour when the sun rises, you will keep watch alone in the forest.

"The rest of the pack will sleep. We will put our trust in you. We will depend upon you to warn us of danger. If an attack on us by men is threatened, then your warning will save our lives. This is your task. Do you understand?"

"I understand."

"Do you accept the challenge?"

"I accept."

"Very well. Go now, eat and rest. Prepare yourself for your vigil."

CHAPTER 13

Craig sat alone in the forest at the dead of night. The first fear of being left by himself in such an unfamiliar place had passed.

The other wolves had melted quietly away into the trees, leaving him unsure whether they were watching him from a distance, or had in truth gone to sleep and put their trust in him to guard them.

He was amazed at how quickly they could hide themselves. At only a few paces, their grizzled brown and grey coats blended perfectly with the tree trunks and undergrowth.

For such large animals, they moved amazingly quietly, passing close by without so much as a panting breath to disclose their whereabouts.

No wonder men feared them, he thought. They must seem to move like ghosts in the night, silent and invisible.

The weight of responsibility Nurek had put upon him to stand guard over the pack had, at first, frightened the life out of him, but now he felt better about it. The longer he sat at his post, the calmer he felt.

Sounds carried a great distance in the clear air and he felt sure even he, unpractised as he was, would pick up warning noises in good time to raise the alarm.

"I can do this," he told himself, settling down beside a sturdy tree, feeling the thick carpet of pine needles making a cushion under him.

He found he was responding to the silence of the wild forest, the pitch black sky, and the pine scented breeze, with a kind of excitement he had not expected.

He was unused to being so still for as long as this. To remain in one place, wide awake and senses alert, was a new experience for him.

With hours to do nothing but sit and listen, he gradually tuned in to all the minute rustlings among the pine needles, as insects and small forest animals woke and began to move about.

As he watched in ever-increasing wonder, the black velvet of the sky showed itself sprinkled with tiny points of light. The longer he looked, the more stars he could see, until the sky didn't seem dark at all, but bright with millions of tiny sparks.

Craig felt strengthened and empowered by what he could sense around him. He wanted to run with the wild wolves. He wanted Nurek's trust. He would do anything he asked him.

Gradually, the inky blackness of the night lightened, first to grey and then, little-by-little to a pearly flush, tinged with the softest pink.

In the earliest dawn, the stars began to fade, the smallest and most distant first, until only the brightest defied the lustre of the new day.

Eventually, they were all gone as full light flooded the sky.

From the shadows, Nurek had observed the little stranger sitting, alert and vigilant, beside his tree through the night, his watchfulness unwavering, his concentration profound.

Nurek nodded, pleased with his protégé. The young one had completed his first task. Nurek stepped forward.

"You have done well. You are released from your duty."

Gratefully, Craig got up and stretched himself.

He turned to look at Nurek who spoke again:

"Today we hunt. You will come with us. We will

teach you the ways of our pack. You are now one of

us."

CHAPTER 14

Although he was flattered to be included in the hunting party, Craig found it terribly hard work. He was not used to this amount of exercise, and certainly not on four legs.

Nurek had hand-picked his fastest runners and they ran for miles at great speed. Soon Craig was exhausted.

He had been put with the other young wolves, occupying the central position in the pack. They were surrounded by older and more experienced hunters, with a couple of veterans bringing up the rear, to ensure that none of the beginners slipped behind.

Craig was very glad of their support as he

felt himself dropping back, unable to keep up the unflagging pace set by the leaders.

When they realised he could not go on, the rear-guard called for a break and, indeed, all the youngsters were glad. Craig was sure they would have gone on until they dropped, rather than be the first to quit, but they were all happy to take advantage of the opportunity to sprawl, panting, on the ground.

When they set off again, the pace was not so fast.

Craig wondered, as he jogged along in the middle of the pack, whether he would have the strength to hunt a deer after all this, if they ever found one.

He did not have a great deal longer to wait before they stopped again, this time in more open grassland.

Scouts had been sent ahead and a herd of deer had been sighted.

The plan was to observe them for a while and select the most likely victim for their attack. They wanted as big an animal as they could take, as there were many mouths to feed, but that meant picking out an old or weak-looking specimen who would not put up much of a fight.

As the youngsters sat listening to the strategy being discussed, well hidden among what cover there was, the deer came into view.

Craig's heart pounded as he caught his first sight of them. They were beautiful – golden coloured and sleek, with long, delicate legs and huge dark eyes. They seemed to be either pregnant or mothers with small calves. His resolve faltered.

Hungry he might be, wolf he might have become, but kill one of these?

He didn't think he could do it.

In the event, Craig's loyalty to the pack was not put into question.

The younger wolves were there to look and learn. The attack was mounted by the expert hunters who had done this many times before and could be relied upon to carry out the assassination with speed and efficiency. Craig shut his eyes as they seized upon their target and was very glad that it was all over swiftly.

He dared not let Nurek see that he was reluctant to join in the celebrations after the kill, so he quickly gobbled up the morsel he was given. The rest of the carcass would be dragged home to share with the other members of the pack who had remained back in the clearing by the cabin.

CHAPTER 15

The return journey didn't seem so bad. Although they had a long way to go through the forest, they were under no pressure of speed now, and Craig found he was actually enjoyed the scenery, looking all around and taking in the sights and sounds of the criss-crossing tracks and green shady dells.

The day was pleasantly warm with a breeze. There were streams wending their way through the wood, so they could stop for a drink as often as they wished.

It was getting dark as they began the last lap of their journey. They were tramping along quietly now, spread out in a long straggling line, walking singly or in twos. They were all looking forward to getting home.

Nurek, who was at the head of the troop, and a watchman bringing up the rear, kept a constant look-out, aware that now was the time of greatest danger, when energy levels were at their lowest, and the end of the road was in sight.

It was Nurek himself who gave a sudden signal that brought them all to a halt, and caused them to strain eyes and ears for danger signs. Craig could detect nothing but the wolves could. They were all on the alert, and there was no doubt that they could hear something.

"Men," announced Nurek, "over there." He gestured ahead and to the left. Craig still couldn't hear anything.

"There are many of them. They are heading towards our clearing," Nurek continued.

"They are close to our base. This is what we will do. We will spread out into a circle, from here, going behind the group of men, so we will surround them. Then we will frighten them away. We do not want them near our home."

The wolves immediately began to break ranks, one of the older ones each taking one of the youngsters with them. They slipped away noiselessly between the trees. Nurek turned to Craig.

"I have a special task for you."

Craig stiffened, wondering what he would be told to do, and hoping this was not punishment for his cowardice when the deer was killed. He had better listen carefully to Nurek and be sure he understood his instructions.

"Run as fast as you can to the cabin in the clearing and wake Garell and the old warrior who sleeps his days away there.

"Tell them men are coming and they have to go into the woods. We need them to help us drive the men away. Use your legs. Run!"

Craig took off as fast as he could down the track between the pine trees. It couldn't be far, surely. They were nearly home when Nurek raised the alarm. He tore along, determined to carry out his instructions to the letter, not to let Nurek down.

Craig knew Garell would not hesitate to take the cubs outside into the undergrowth and ensure they were safely out of danger. But would the old wolf obey him? He would have to tell him the orders came from Nurek, then, surely, he would.

He could see the clearing opening up ahead of him, and the silhouette of the log cabin looming up. He put on a last spurt and skidded into the clearing, gasping for breath. It took all his weight to push the door open. The bigger wolves had no trouble with it.

"Quick," he shouted, "You must leave. Nurek has sent me to warn you. You have to go outside."

"What is the matter?" Garell jumped up anxiously, and gathered the cubs to her.

"Men . . . men are coming. You have to go outside, Nurek said so."

Without another word, Garell swept up the cubs and was gone.

CHAPTER 16

"Come on . . . you've got to go too!" Craig told the other wolf. "You've got to leave!"

His message was totally ignored. The old fellow continued to snore away, making no more response than flicking his ears in his sleep.

Craig tried again:

"There are men on the way here and Nurek needs your help to frighten them away. He says you must go into the forest."

Nothing.

He wasn't sure how far he dared go with physical efforts to rouse the old wolf. If Lurrar took offence and snapped at him, he would come off very much the worse. Even a cuff round the head from one of those massive paws would knock him over.

But he had to do something.

He went round behind Lurrar's head, where Lurrar wouldn't be able to reach him easily, and took hold of one of Lurrar's ears.

He counted one . . . two . . . three . . . and then bit, and beat a hasty retreat backwards, as Lurrar shook his head angrily. But his reaction was short-lived. He gave a huge snort, turned over and went back to sleep.

Desperate measures were clearly needed. Craig looked round for inspiration. All he could see was the three-legged stool. He went and grabbed it in his teeth.

He was reluctant to use violence on such a respected elder of the pack, but there seemed no option.

He swung the stool and hit Lurrar with it as hard as he could.

The shock was enough to bring Lurrar leaping to his feet. Before Craig could move out of his way, he found himself confronting the largest set of teeth he had ever seen, bared in a menacing growl.

Scared as he was, Craig held his ground:

"Lurrar. Don't be angry. I had to wake you. Nurek sent me. There are men coming and Nurek says you must leave the cabin and join him outside. He has work for you to do."

Lurrar tossed his great head and Craig felt the spittle from his jaws on his face but he stood stock still, facing him out.

"You are either very brave, or very foolish, to disturb my peace," Lurrar rumbled.

"Nurek sent me. He says you must go outside."

Craig would not be deflected, willing him to

move, to go . . . just go.

"Nurek?" Lurar repeated, in a strange voice.

"Nurek. Our leader."

"I was once leader of this pack," Lurrar said slowly.

"Yes. I know. And now Nurek needs your help. He has a job to do and he can't do it without you. Lurrar! Go outside and help Nurek now!"

"He needs me, does he? Well, well, well."

Lurrar shook his head again, as if trying to clear his brain. He turned clumsily towards the door and Craig saw he had a severe limp. One of his back legs seemed paralysed and dragged behind him as he walked.

Craig doubted the old wolf would make it to the door unaided, never mind across the clearing.

"Don't be offended, Lurrar," he said, "but I think you might find it easier if you lean on me."

The weight of the venerable old wolf was almost too much for him, but he braced himself to support him. Little by little, they struggled across to the door.

Between them, they managed to push it open. As they edged out into the clearing, they could plainly hear the noise of the men crashing through the forest, and see their lanterns.

Although the shelter of the trees was only a few paces away, they had to stop several times. Craig hoped he would be able to hold the old leader up long enough to get there.

At last they reached safety, and Lurrar dragged himself into the undergrowth, where his coat blended into the shadows so that even at such a short distance, he was unlikely to be detected.

Whatever it was Nurek wanted Lurrar to do, Craig hoped he could do it from here, because he couldn't get him any further away from the hut.

"Will you be all right here, Lurrar?"

"Yes. I will not be seen. But you, little friend, your pale fur shines like a beacon in the moonlight. You will be seen. Run back quickly into the cabin and hide."

Craig turned as the first of the men came bursting through the trees and with a quick nod of thanks to Lurrar, bounded for the cabin and flung himself through the door.

No sooner was he inside than he heard a heavy object land against the door behind him, something he assumed one of the men had thrown.

"Just in time!" he thought.

He burrowed down into Lurrar's pile of dead leaves and waited to find out what the wolf pack was going to do.

CHAPTER 17

It was a few moments before he heard it. To begin with, he didn't realise what it was. As he listened, a distant, low, moaning tone began to rise in both pitch and volume. It went on and on, getting louder and louder as it slid up the scale, a blend of full-throated voices giving vent to a spine-chilling howl.

It raised the hackles on the back of his neck, tingled in his blood, echoed round and round in his head.

Before the first howl had reached its crescendo, another had begun, nearer than the first, even more eerie, other-worldly.

Another howl began, closer still, just the other side of the cabin wall. Lurrar and Garell were adding their voices to the cacophony, sending a message of dread to the men who had dared to invade their territory.

Craig understood now. The wolves had no need to fight the men. They would drive them away by giving voice to a sound that conjured up in men a primeval fear. It would be enough. No blood would be shed, but the dominance of the wolf pack would be re-established in these woods.

What a defeatist he had been, to think the men could get the better of the pack. If he was outside he would probably be able to hear them running away now, bumping into the trees in their haste to get away from the clearing.

Ha! He would love to see that! He ran to the door to nudge it open, but it wouldn't move. Then he remembered the log, or whatever it was, that had landed against the door just after he dashed inside. It must have wedged the door shut.

He would have to wait until Nurek and the others came back and moved it out of the way before he could go outside.

Turning back from the door, he noticed a flicker of lantern-light through the high window. Someone must still be nearby. In fact, the people outside must be very close to the cabin because the light was getting brighter.

What kind of men would be foolish enough to stay here, surrounded by baying wolves?

He paced round the hut, quickly returning to the door, and then he caught a whiff that filled him with fear.

Creeping under the door he saw the first tendrils of smoke.

The light outside was not from lanterns – the cabin was on fire!

He threw himself at the door with all his might but it would not budge. The timber was old and dry, already it was beginning to crackle as it caught, like tinder. In no time at all the whole building was ablaze.

He had to get out, but what could he do. The door was jammed shut. The window was much too far up in the wall for him to get to – even Nurek would not have been able to reach it on his hind legs. All was lost.

As this thought weighed down on him, a picture of his sister's face floated into his mind. Lisa! He had to get back to Lisa.

Confused by the heat and flames and billowing smoke, he tried to focus his mind.

Wasn't there a window in the hut? Opposite the door. But high up. Too high to reach, right?

He looked again, and was surprised to see that the window-frame was no longer where it had been before. As the timber burned away, so the window-frame had slipped down, hanging at a crazy angle, much lower than before.

He glanced up. The roof was alight. It would not be long now before it caved in on him. He knew it was futile to even think of it. But if there was a one-in-a-million chance of escape, he had to try.

He reached once more for the three-legged stool and dragged it over part-way towards the window. Then he backed away as far as he dared towards the burning wall behind him.

Judging the distance as best he could, he took a run of a few paces, leapt up on to the stool and launched himself at the window-frame, as the first of the roof timbers dropped down in a crackling shower of sparks.

Outside, the wolves could see what was happening. The long-drawn out howls had given way to tormented, melancholy wailing.

As Craig jumped, he could hear their voices close by, surrounding the blazing hut – the anguished farewell of the wolf pack to one of its own.

CHAPTER 18

Craig was so hot, he was burning up. Had his bid for freedom from the flaming hut been in vain? Had he fallen back into the fiery embers, that even now were consuming him?

He lay where he was, eyes tightly shut, breathless, panting. A bright, white light and an insistent drumming sound were all that filled his tormented brain.

As his swirling thoughts gradually slowed, so, too did the drumming sound. It became more a tap, tap, tap, repeated over and over.

In the furthest back region of his brain he

heard his name: "Craig! Craig!" over and over again.

"Craig! Craig! Open the door!"

The door – it was wedged shut, he couldn't get it open, he couldn't get out of the hut, couldn't escape.

Panic flooded over him again. He kicked out. Something was tied round his legs. He couldn't move. What was happening?

He half-opened his eyes. Close up to him he could see the familiar faces of the wolf pack. It was as if his friends had gathered round him to say one last goodbye.

He sank back, exhausted, willing himself gone from this impossible situation.

"Craig! Craig! Open the door!"

It was his sister's voice. Lisa. He roused himself – agitated, not knowing where he was. He couldn't move his legs.

What was happening? His heart pounded with anxiety.

"Craig! Can you hear me?"

It was definitely Lisa's voice. Yes, he could hear her. Where was he?

Suddenly, he was fully awake. He was in his bedroom, lying fully dressed on his bed. He was completely entangled in his duvet cover so that he could hardly move.

Lisa was tapping on the door.

"Wake up, Craig, and move the chair!"

He stumbled out of bed, still half entwined in the duvet cover. He dragged the chair out from under the door handle and flopped down on the bed again.

Lisa opened the door and came in.

"The power's come back on, so Auntie Shirl's made us all a cup of tea. I brought yours up. Here it is."

Lisa put down his mug of tea on the bedside table and left the room.

Craig could only nod his thanks. His heart was still racing and he couldn't catch his breath. He kicked his legs free of his duvet cover and spread it out on the bed beside him.

Nurek. Garell. Lurrar. They were all there, with the rest of the pack, with their grey fur and those yellow eyes that followed him everywhere. He was of their kind. He was one of them.

He didn't want to be back with Auntie Shirl and Uncle Pete and their constant quarrelling.

Craig gathered up the rumpled duvet cover into his arms and hugged it tightly to him. And he wept.